THE
BRASS RING
NANCY TAFURI

GREENWILLOW BOOKS • NEW YORK

For Cristina

The carousel pictured in this book is
The Flying Horse Carousel in Watch
Hill, Rhode Island, one of the oldest
carousels in the United States.

Colored pencils, watercolors, and a
black pen were used for the full-color
art. The text type is Adobe Garamond.

Printed in Singapore by Tien Wah Press
First Edition   10 9 8 7 6 5 4 3 2 1

Library of Congress
Cataloging-in-Publication Data

Tafuri, Nancy.
The brass ring / by Nancy Tafuri.
    p.   cm.
Summary: Being on vacation is even
more fun for one who is bigger and can
do more things such as ride a bike, float
and swim, and buy a carousel ticket.
ISBN 0-688-14168-4 (trade).
ISBN 0-688-14169-2 (lib. bdg.)
[1. Vacations—Fiction.
2. Growth—Fiction.
3. Size—Fiction.]   I. Title.
PZ7.T117Br   1996   [E]—dc20
95-25084   CIP   AC

I like being big. When I was little, I really didn't know what vacations were. I would sleep in the car instead of asking, "Are we there yet?"

When I was little,
I couldn't say hello
to everyone when
we arrived or
run to the beach.

Now I can ride
my bicycle and
meet new friends.

When I was little,
I couldn't float on
my back or swim.

I couldn't
race a wave
or build a
sand castle.

Now that I am big,
I can find
sea stars and
snails.

I can dig
for clams and
scoop up
rock crabs.

But now what I like best
about vacations is the carousel.

Now I am big enough
to buy my own ticket.

I stand in line until my
favorite outside horse is free.

He is white and silver
with a red saddle.
I call him Thunder.

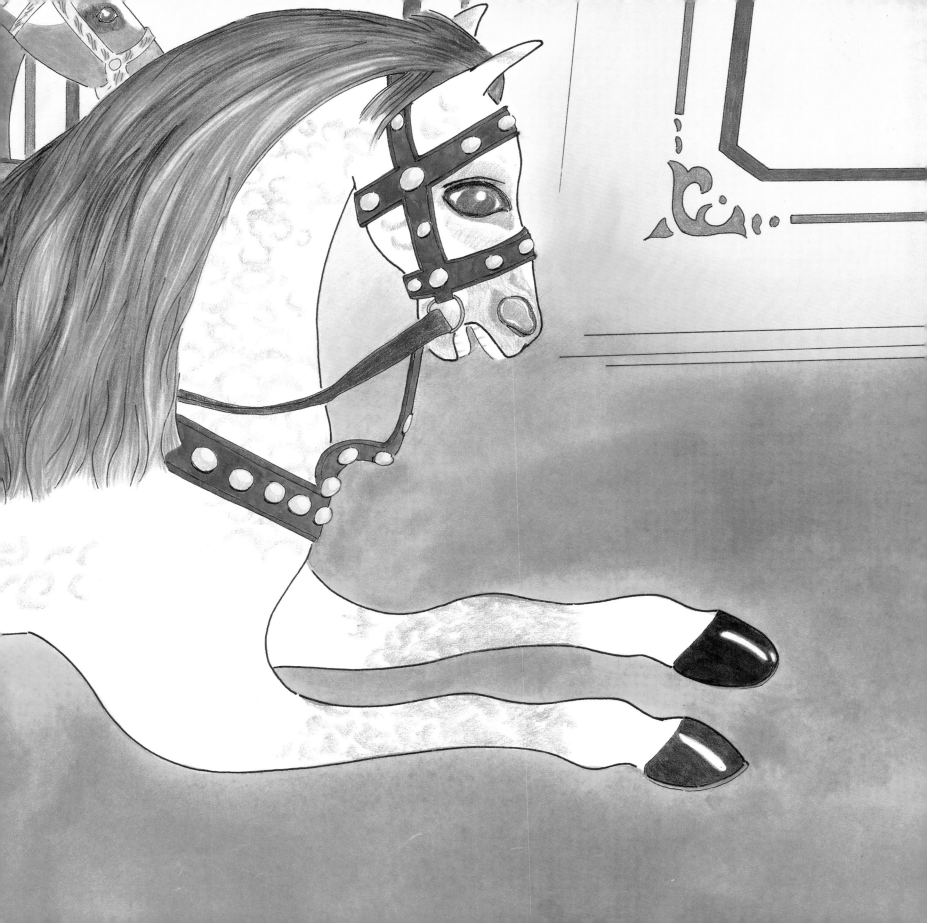

The music starts.
I hold the pole and
ride like the wind!

I watch for the
brass ring and
lean out far.
Can I get it?

I like being BIG !